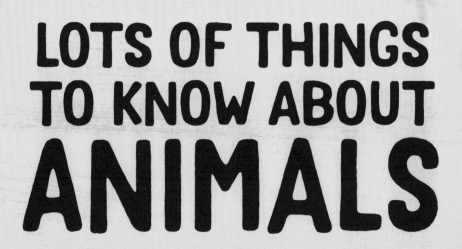

LOTS OF THINGS TO KNOW ABOUT ANIMALS

James Maclaine

Illustrated by
Carolina Búzio

Designed by
Katie Webb

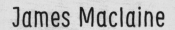

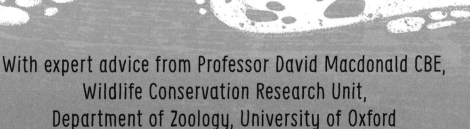

With expert advice from Professor David Macdonald CBE,
Wildlife Conservation Research Unit,
Department of Zoology, University of Oxford

USBORNE QUICKLINKS

For links to websites where you can watch, listen to and read extra facts about the animals in this book and more, go to
usborne.com/Quicklinks
and type in the title of this book.

You can also download a map of the world at Usborne Quicklinks if you want to find any of the places mentioned on the following pages.

Please follow the internet safety guidelines at Usborne Quicklinks. Children should be supervised online.

Did you know that if you zoomed in on a butterfly's wings, you'd see thousands of tiny scales?

Wow! But what are SCALES?

You can check the meaning of that word in the glossary on page 62. And there's an index on pages 63-64 to help you search for a topic.

Ocean giants

Of all the creatures that have ever lived on Earth, blue whales are the largest. But how **big** are their body parts?

A blue whale's eyeball is about the size of a grapefruit.

Its tail is as wide as a football net.

Each flipper is longer than a bed.

Its heart is as big as a bumper car.

Its tongue is as heavy as five grand pianos.

3

The baby animal that's LARGER than its parents

Almost all animals are much, much *bigger* than their babies.

Check the number under each adult to see how much heavier it is than its newborn baby.

SNOWY OWL

LLAMA

PYTHON

10 TIMES

20 TIMES

40 TIMES

Snowy owl chicks are similar in size to small oranges.

But there are frogs in the Amazon Rainforest, called paradoxical frogs, whose babies aren't so small...

The frogs lay eggs that hatch into tadpoles, which grow almost *four times* bigger than the adult frogs.

A newborn panda weighs about the same as an apple.

GIANT PANDA

It takes at least 30 years for sea turtles to become fully grown.

LOGGERHEAD SEA TURTLE

LEOPARD

900
TIMES

6,750
TIMES

80
TIMES

Baby leopard cubs are six times smaller than adult pet cats.

You're such a BIG baby!

As they grow up, paradoxical frog tadpoles sprout legs, lose their tails and *shrink*.

How to spot a leopard...   ...from a jaguar

Leopards and jaguars are types of big cats with big, splotchy spots. To tell them apart, you just need to examine their markings...

Both leopards and jaguars have splotches shaped like flowers. They are called **rosettes**.

LEOPARD

JAGUAR

But only the rosettes on a jaguar's fur have little spots inside them.

Why horses dress up like zebras

Some animals are less likely to suffer insect bites than others. For instance, zebras...

Their stripes **dazzle** flies, so they can't see where to land and bite.

BZZZ

OUCH!

It's much easier for flies to attack horses...

...**unless** they're wearing a rug.

BZZZ

You can't bite us.

And the **best** rugs for stopping flies have black and white stripes.

Octopuses in disguise

Most octopuses can change the way their skin looks to match the ocean floor.

This helps them to hide from sharks and other hunters...

...as well as the sea creatures that they try to hunt.

Common octopuses sometimes cover their bodies with seashells to keep out of sight.

Veined octopuses carry two coconut halves...

...so they can hide inside them.

HAVE YOU SEEN THIS OCTOPUS?

It's a mimic octopus. This type of octopus scares away hunters by **pretending** to be poisonous animals.

It can make the shape of a flatfish, called a...

BANDED SOLE

It fans out its arms to match the spines of a...

LIONFISH

It wiggles just two arms and hides the rest of its body beneath the sand, so it looks like this snake.

SEA KRAIT

How tiny ants are actually STRONGER than gorillas

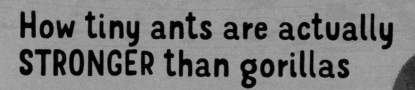

To find out which animals are stronger than which, you could compare how much they **weigh** with how much they can **carry**...

Harpy eagles are strong enough to snatch monkeys that weigh the **same** as them.

Tigers use their powerful jaws to drag cows **twice** as heavy as themselves.

Gorillas are strong enough to lift **four** times their own weight.

The muscles in gorillas' arms are bigger than in their legs. That's what makes them such great weightlifters.

WORLD'S STRONGEST ANIMAL COMPETITION

But some of the smallest animals on Earth can carry **even more**.

Leafcutter ants pick up pieces of leaves that each weigh as much as **20** ants.

50 TIMES

They carry the pieces to their nests.

20 TIMES

And there are dung beetles that can roll balls of poo **50** times heavier than their own body weight.

Dung beetles collect animals' poo to eat and lay their eggs in.

I can't even lift half my body weight.

How HIGH can birds and bumblebees fly?

The highest-flying birds are Rüppell's vultures. They can soar at heights of 11,300m (37,000ft).

That's as high up as a plane.

Scientists have proved that bumblebees can fly higher than the peak of Mount Everest — the **highest** mountain in the world.

HEIGHT: 8,849m (29,032ft)

When you hear bees buzz, you're actually listening to their wings flap — 200 times every second.

BUZZZ

BUZZZ

BUZZZ

How LOW can sea creatures go?

Enormous cracks in the ocean floor, called trenches, are the deepest places on Earth. They're *pitch black* and *freezing cold*, but some animals live inside them...

This scary-looking creature is an anglerfish. It has a spine dangling from the front of its head that glows in the dark. Little fish are attracted to the light, and the anglerfish gobbles them up.

Snailfish swim *deeper* than any other types of fish. They have soft, jelly-like bodies.

And even at the bottom of the very deepest trenches, there are tube-shaped creatures called sea cucumbers.

The secret of hornbills' nests

Hornbills are strange-looking birds with unusually big beaks. Even more bizarre are the steps they take to lay their eggs...

First, a mother hornbill finds a tree with a large hole in its trunk.

The father brings mud to the hole.

Together, they build a wall that traps the mother inside for **months**.

Here are some more animals with *amazing* nests...

Mother alligators make nests out of rotting plants.

The eggs in the **warmer** parts of the nest hatch into males...

...and the eggs in **cooler** parts hatch into females.

Don't worry! There's a slit in the mud wall so the father can pass the mother things to eat.

Safe in the nest, the mother lays her eggs and waits for them to hatch.

There's a nest on a cliff in Greenland that birds called gyrfalcons have used for more than 2,500 years.

My great, great, great, great, great, great granny hatched up here.

Paradise fish blow lots of tiny **bubbles** to make nests that float.

Incredible!

15

The great shell swap

Most crabs have a hard shell around a soft body, but hermit crabs are a little different. Because they can't grow shells, every hermit crab has to find an old seashell to live inside instead.

Can you guess what happens when they get too big for their shells?

It's feeling tight in here. Time to find a bigger shell...

When an empty shell washes up on a beach, hermit crabs arrive to check it out...

If the shell looks **too big**, they line up in order of size and **wait**.

What are you all doing?

They're waiting for a BIGGER crab to come along. HERE'S one now!

At last a hermit crab the right fit for the new shell will crawl into it. The crab leaves its old shell for the next in line.

The perfect home!

And then each crab changes its shell for the one in front — until there's one little shell left empty at the end of the line.

Noisy animals you CAN'T hear

Many animals aren't as quiet as they seem. They make sounds that are either **too high** or **too low** for people to hear, such as...

Elephants' low, rumbling sounds travel a long way, even in thick, leafy forests.

Some rats laugh at a very high pitch when they're tickled.

Noisier than planes at take-off, sperm whales are the loudest animals in the world. Luckily for your ears, the clicks they make are far too low for humans to hear.

These frogs' chirps are high enough for them to hear each other over the loud waterfalls where they live.

PLAYLIST: FOR ANIMALS' EARS ONLY

RUMBLES
African forest elephants

GIGGLES
Rats

CLICKS
Sperm whales

CHIRPS
Torrent frogs

I can't hear anything!

That's because these sounds are too high or too low for us.

Treetop choirs

The biggest — and **noisiest** — lemurs on the island of Madagascar are called indris. Every day, groups of them sing from the treetops where they live.

The oldest female and male in each group start a duet. They make high and low notes to the same beat.

EEEYA...
EEEEYA...

EEYA...

Then, other members of their family join in with the song.

EEEYA...
EEEEYA...

EEEYA...

But there comes a time when a young male indri sings **out of tune**.

OHHHHHHHH

He does this when he's ready to leave the group and start his own family.

19

The cave of bats that's busier than New York

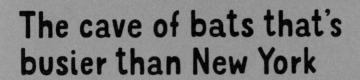

Every summer, lots and lots of bats fly from Mexico to Texas, USA, to have their babies in Bracken Cave.

The bats rest inside during the day. But the adults fly out at night to catch insects.

As the babies grow up, they join the hunt too. This swells the swarm to more than *15 million* bats.

There are twice as many bats in Bracken Cave as there are people in New York — the largest city in America.

Where do the bats go in winter?

They fly back to Mexico, where it's warmer.

Now get ready to join some of the **biggest** crowds of animals on Earth!

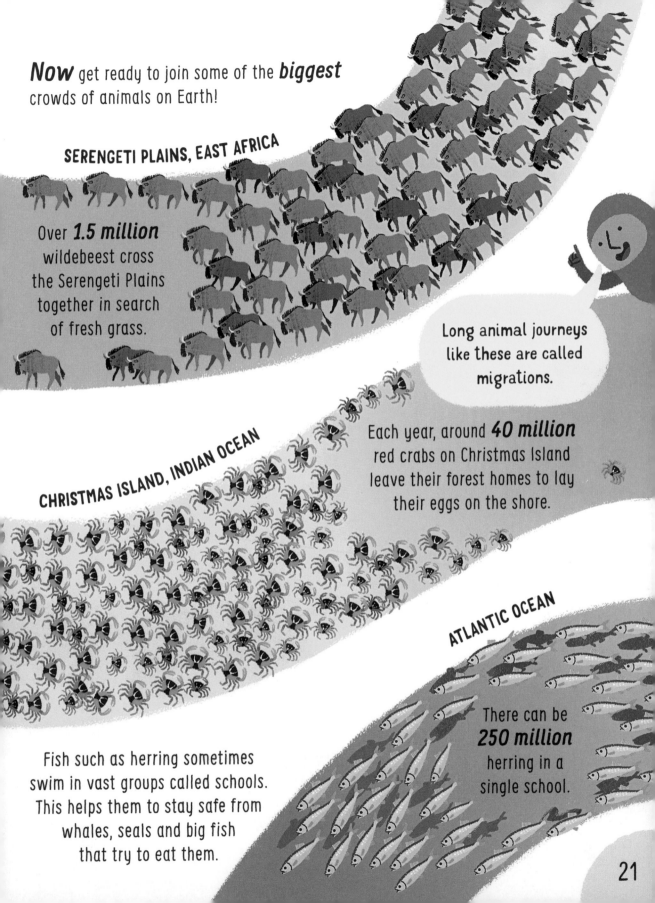

SERENGETI PLAINS, EAST AFRICA

Over **1.5 million** wildebeest cross the Serengeti Plains together in search of fresh grass.

Long animal journeys like these are called migrations.

Each year, around **40 million** red crabs on Christmas Island leave their forest homes to lay their eggs on the shore.

CHRISTMAS ISLAND, INDIAN OCEAN

ATLANTIC OCEAN

There can be **250 million** herring in a single school.

Fish such as herring sometimes swim in vast groups called schools. This helps them to stay safe from whales, seals and big fish that try to eat them.

21

You'll hardly BELIEVE your eyes!

These animals could all steal the show with the *amazing* things they do to impress, confuse or scare each other.

 HOODED SEAL

That's not a red balloon! This is what a male hooded seal looks like when he blows up his inflatable nose.

This strange-looking creature can roll into a near perfect ball. It tucks in its legs and slots its nose snugly beside its tail.

 THREE-BANDED ARMADILLO

 SUPERB BIRD-OF-PARADISE

When this type of bird fans out its feathers, it makes a weird black and turquoise shape that doesn't look like a bird at all.

Springboks are the bounciest show-offs. They leap three times their own height...

...and keep their legs straight.

SPRINGBOK

FRILLED LIZARD

To startle an attacker, this lizard flips up dazzling flaps of skin around its head.

KILLDEER

Why is it pretending to be injured?

This bird seems to have a broken wing... but it's *faking* it.

So hunters try to catch the bird INSTEAD of spotting its babies.

Which live LONGEST?

If you look at the candles on these birthday cakes, you'll find out the record-breaking ages of some of the world's oldest animals.

Happy birthday to you...

185

GIANT TORTOISE

100

COCKATOO

400

GREENLAND SHARK

200

BOWHEAD WHALE

500

OCEAN QUAHOG CLAM

Animals from dinosaur times

The last dinosaurs died a long, long time ago. But a few of the types of creatures that lived alongside them are still around **now**...

DRAGONFLY

MOSQUITO

BEE

COCKROACH

When scientists tested the bones of a T. rex...

...they discovered that **chickens** are some of its closest living relatives.

MILLIPEDE

ANT

25

Why whales blow bubbles

Blowing bubbles can be surprisingly **useful** for groups of humpback whales.

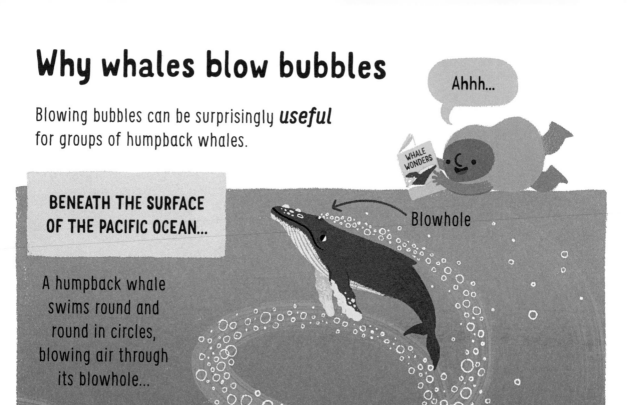

BENEATH THE SURFACE OF THE PACIFIC OCEAN...

Blowhole

A humpback whale swims round and round in circles, blowing air through its blowhole...

...making rings of bubbles.

DEEPER DOWN...

Other whales chase fish into the middle of the bubbles...

The whales use their fins to stop fish from swimming away.

How do prairie dogs say hello?

Prairie dogs are **not** dogs. They're small, furry animals that live together in burrows. But they do bark to warn of danger, and when they meet a prairie dog they know...

Lions **rub** their heads together.

EEEEEEEEEE

EEEEE EEEEEE

Dolphins **whistle**.

Lobsters squirt **wee** at one another from holes in their heads.

A young fox **crouches** low and folds back its ears to greet an adult fox.

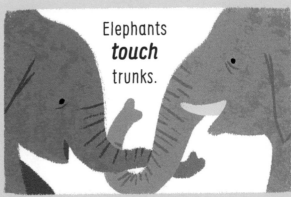

Elephants **touch** trunks.

Chimpanzees share a **hug**.

Dogs **sniff** bottoms. The smells remind them if they've met before.

Why sloths turn green in the rain

Sloths are slow, sleepy creatures. But their shaggy fur is *crawling* with all kinds of living things...

LICE

MOSQUITOS

TICKS

MOTHS

ALGAE

Tiny plants called algae grow in the fur, too. When it rains, the algae turn green — and so does the sloth.

Looking green is a good thing for sloths. It helps them to hide up in the trees.

What makes flamingos pink

When they first hatch out, flamingos are a dull grey.

Their feathers and skin start to turn pink when they eat brine shrimp living in water.

BRINE SHRIMP

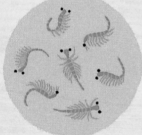

The more shrimp flamingos eat, the **pinker** they become.

SHADES OF FLAMINGO

JUST HATCHED   FLUFFY CLOUD   FIRST FLUSH

PINKING   BLUSH   IN THE PINK

PINKEST

What's that flamingo doing?

It's rubbing oil from the base of its tail onto its feathers. This turns them even pinker.

What's for dinner?

Can you imagine a restaurant where animals could eat?
There'd be some very strange things on the menu...

Blood

You might have heard that vampire bats
bite animals to drink their blood, but did
you know that there are also vampire moths?

Soil

Soil contains salt, which
animals need to keep healthy.

Turtle tears

Tears are salty, too. In the
Amazon Rainforest, butterflies land
on turtles to drink from their eyes.

Chef says
we've run out
of soil!

That's because so many
animals eat it: parrots,
orangutans, elephants, sheep...

Poisonous leaves

The leaves on eucalyptus trees are poisonous for most animals – except koalas. Their stomachs can break down the poisons safely.

Old skin

Lizards shed their skin. Sometimes, they swallow the pieces they tear off.

Fresh poo

Guinea pigs and rabbits eat any soft poos that they do because they still contain stuff that's good for them.

Half-eaten meat

Wolves bring up food from their tummies for young wolves. This makes it soft enough for them to eat.

Animal life in a land of ice

Brrrrr! Even in summer, many parts of the Antarctic are chillier than a kitchen freezer. So how do the animals here stay alive and warm?

Penguins have layers of different feathers.

EMPEROR PENGUINS

Emperor penguins rock back on the heels of their feet to stop their toes from freezing in the snow.

ADÉLIE PENGUINS

Stiff feathers on top are waterproof.

Fluffy feathers close to their skin trap heat.

If a breathing hole starts to freeze over, they use their teeth to chomp through any slush.

When they need to pop up for air, they find holes in the ice.

WEDDELL SEAL

Seals spend as many as nine out of every ten hours swimming under the ice.

CRABEATER SEAL

Blubber keeps seals warm when they're hunting fish and squid far below the surface – where the water is **even** cooler.

SOUTHERN ELEPHANT SEAL

Southern elephant seals dive deepest. They can hold their breath for almost **two hours**.

Seals look chubby because they have a very thick layer of fat under their skin called **blubber**.

That's because their blood contains special antifreeze.

These fish don't look very blubbery... How come they don't freeze?

The animal that would win a marathon

A marathon is a running race over 42km (26 miles) long.

Cheetahs reach the fastest speeds of any animals on land, but they can't keep going over long distances — so they'd be no good in marathons.

Horses can run fast and far. They'd finish a marathon in two and a half hours. That's as fast as the best human athletes.

Camels are even better marathon runners than horses.

I'd reach the finish line after one hour only.

And thanks to their long, powerful legs, ostriches would be the *winners*.

Finish time:

45 MINUTES

SURPRISING swimmers

The animals on this page spend most of their lives on the ground or up trees, but they're all impressively strong swimmers too.

TIGERS
Unlike many other types of cats, tigers enjoy getting wet.

ELEPHANTS

I use my trunk as a snorkel to breathe.

SLOTHS
Sloths are three times faster in water than on land.

PIGS
Pigs can swim long distances to cross rivers.

The animals' tool kit

Did you know that some animals are so clever that they've learned how to use tools?

Check out what's inside their tool kit on these pages.

Thirsty chimpanzees scoop up water with leaves.

STICKS

LEAVES

If a puffin has an itch, it picks up a stick to scratch itself.

Monkeys called long-tailed macaques clean their teeth with feathers.

FEATHERS

TOP TOOLS FOR ANIMALS

Asian elephants hold branches in their trunks and swing them to swat bothersome flies.

Woodpecker finches use spines from spiky cactus plants to prise tasty insects out from cracks.

Natural sponges grow on the sea floor.

Some dolphins pluck them to wear on their noses so they can dig for fish in rocky sand without getting scratched.

Capuchin monkeys smash nuts out of their shells by hammering them with big stones.

BRANCHES

CACTUS SPINES

SPONGES

STONES

39

You'll never guess why pandas do handstands...

You may want to pinch your nose, because things are about to get very, very **smelly**...

Pandas use all kinds of smells to send messages to each other and show where they live.

They leave piles of dung for other pandas to sniff.

Aha - a female panda lives nearby.

They make smells under their tails and rub them onto rocks and trees.

And male pandas have found another way to spread their smells around too.

They stand on their front paws next to a tree...

...and spray their strong-smelling wee high up its trunk.

This tells other male pandas to STAY AWAY.

...and what shape poos wombats do

If you think animal poo is yucky, *look away now*.

WOMBAT

Wombats' poos are unlike any other animal's — they're cube-shaped.

ELEPHANT

A ball of elephant dung is about the size of a cauliflower.

BLUE WHALE

Blue whale poo is bright orange, and just one blue whale poo would fill about 20 buckets.

PARROTFISH

Parrotfish grind rock-like coral into tiny pieces when they eat. So, when they poo, sand comes out.

HIPPO

Hippos spin their tails to spray their dung far and wide.

Animal architects

Small animals make great builders, when it comes to designing and constructing places to live.

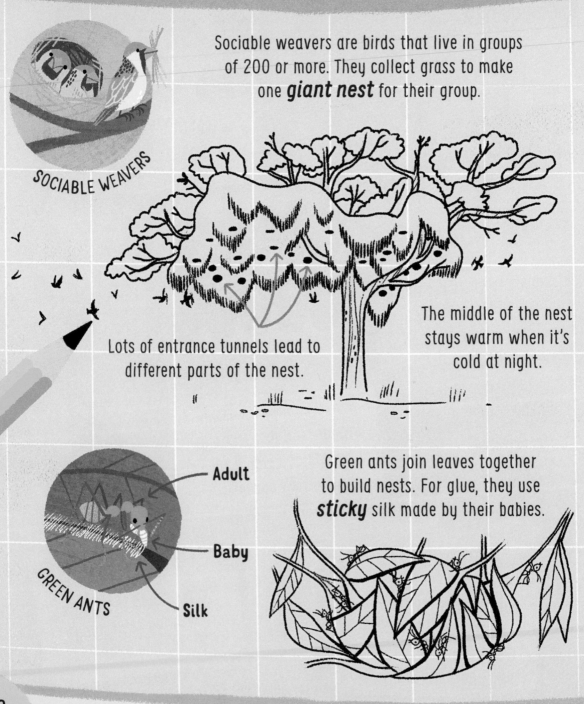

SOCIABLE WEAVERS

Sociable weavers are birds that live in groups of 200 or more. They collect grass to make one *giant nest* for their group.

Lots of entrance tunnels lead to different parts of the nest.

The middle of the nest stays warm when it's cold at night.

GREEN ANTS

Adult

Baby

Silk

Green ants join leaves together to build nests. For glue, they use *sticky* silk made by their babies.

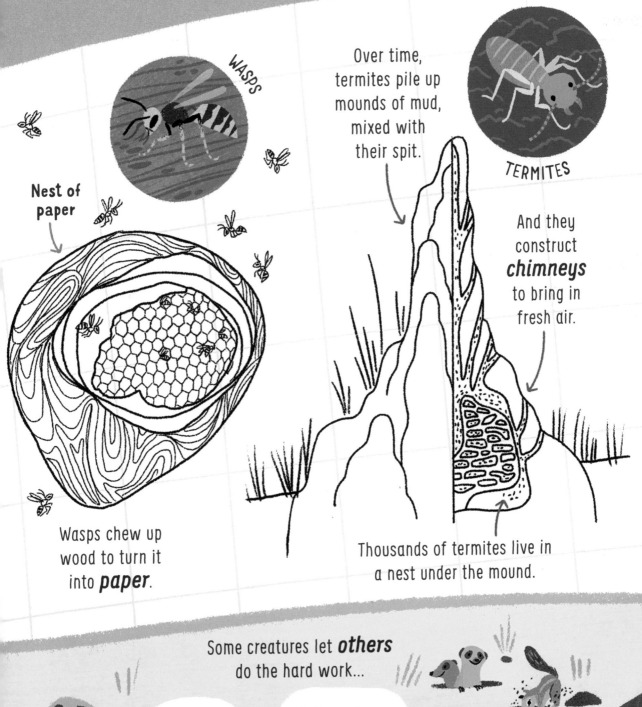

WASPS

Over time, termites pile up mounds of mud, mixed with their spit.

TERMITES

Nest of paper

And they construct **chimneys** to bring in fresh air.

Wasps chew up wood to turn it into **paper**.

Thousands of termites live in a nest under the mound.

Some creatures let **others** do the hard work...

Thanks for building our home, ground squirrel.

You're welcome, meerkat.

Meerkats move into burrows, dug by ground squirrels or mongooses.

43

Walking on water

Lizards mostly live on land, but there are a few types that can do some amazing things in water.

This basilisk lizard can run across rivers without **sinking**.

Flaps of skin between its toes keep it afloat.

Marine iguanas are the only lizards that live in the sea.

After swimming, they get rid of salty seawater from their bodies by sneezing.

Aaachooooooooooooooooooooooooooooooo

Little lizards called water anoles blow bubbles that stick to their heads.

This gives them air to breathe underwater for over 15 minutes.

Snakes in the air

Snakes don't have wings, but some can appear to **fly** between trees. They are called flying snakes.

First, a flying snake pushes itself off a branch.

Then, it wiggles its body and makes itself flat to **glide** through the air.

Hey! All of these different animals can glide too...

Yes, and spiders shoot silk threads to catch a breeze, which carries them through the air.

FLYING SQUIRREL

GLIDING FROG

FLYING SQUID

Whodunit

Beware thieves!
The animals in this line-up
are all known to **steal**...

Spotted hyenas do hunt for
themselves, but sometimes they
snatch food from wild dogs.

SPOTTED HYENA

LION

Adult male lions work alone.
A single lion can steal food from
a gang of hyenas all for himself.

These sea birds wait for other birds to catch fish, then they attack.

GREAT SKUA

Wasps raid honey bees' nests to eat their honey.

WASPS

These penguins pinch stones from each other.

CHINSTRAP PENGUINS

Raccoons rob the nests of birds, turtles and alligators, to find eggs to eat.

RACCOON

Do penguins steal stones to eat them?

No – they use them to build nests.

47

How baby swifts get ready to cross continents

At the start of summer, swifts fly from Africa to parts of Asia and Europe. When they get there, they make nests in cracks and crevices where they lay their eggs.

After hatching, swift chicks only have one or two months to grow up. Then it's time to leave their nest and go on the **extraordinarily long** journey to Africa **non-stop**.

Are their wings strong enough to fly such a long way?

Yes! They practise with press-ups inside the nest.

48

The birds that fly further than astronauts

Of all the birds on Earth, Arctic terns fly *furthest*.

ARCTIC TERN

ARCTIC

ANTARCTIC

Every year, as summer ends in the Arctic, they fly to the Antarctic — where summer is just beginning. And when summer ends there, they fly *back!*

Arctic terns make this incredible journey because they need bright, sunny days to hunt fish.

In its lifetime, an Arctic tern can fly more than 2.4 million km (1.5 million miles) – that's about the same as three trips to and from the Moon.

49

Old and new body parts

Lots of animals lose hairs, scales, teeth, claws and other parts of their bodies throughout their lives. But often they grow back.

Sharks have hundreds of teeth in rows. Whenever a tooth drops out, it's replaced by the one growing behind it.

In its lifetime, a single shark can grow as many as **30,000** teeth.

As they get older, snakes, crabs and spiders shed the outer layer of their bodies in *one piece*.

Every year, the antlers on male deer's heads fall off.

Each male starts growing a new pair just a few weeks later.

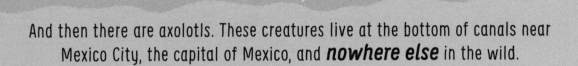

And then there are axolotls. These creatures live at the bottom of canals near Mexico City, the capital of Mexico, and **nowhere else** in the wild.

Those frilly parts behind an axolotl's head help it to breathe. They're called gills.

Big fish live here, too, and sometimes, while trying to catch an axolotl, they bite one of its legs right off.

Uh oh...

But the whole leg will grow back — toes and all.

It can take several weeks or months for an axolotl to regrow all the skin, muscles and bones that make up its leg.

51

First aid for orangutans

Orangutans live in trees, but climbing up trunks, swinging between branches and carrying young orangutans can make their arms *ache*. They can't visit a doctor – so what do they do?

OUCH...

OW

Orangutans search for a type of plant that they *never* eat.

But they chew its leaves to make a foamy lotion...

...which they spit out and rub into sore parts of their bodies.

What's so good about these leaves?

They contain chemicals that SOOTHE pain.

FIRST AID

KEEP BACK!

These three animals have one thing in common — they all use a type of poison called **venom**.

A stingray is a type of fish. It whips its tail to inject venom through a long spine.

STINGRAY

PLATYPUS

Male platypuses have spikes on their back legs to sting with venom.

SPITTING COBRA

Some snakes shoot venom from their fangs.

DON'T TOUCH!

This bird's feathers and this frog's skin are both covered in poison.

WARNING HOODED PITOHUI

DANGER GOLDEN DART FROG

Scientists think that their poison comes from all the poisonous beetles and ants that they eat.

If they stopped eating these insects, they would become *less poisonous*.

How animals make art

The starburst design inside this frame is as pretty as a painting. But the artists who create these patterns live under the sea.

Patterns like this are made in the sandy sea floor, near Japan, by male white-spotted pufferfish.

It takes each fish about a week to create his work of art. He shapes the sand with his fins and clears away any untidy stones with his mouth.

WHITE-SPOTTED PUFFERFISH

Why do the male pufferfish go to all that effort?

To impress females, so they can have babies together.

54

Male bowerbirds also take great care to get the attention of females. They arrange sticks into intricate structures, called **bowers**.

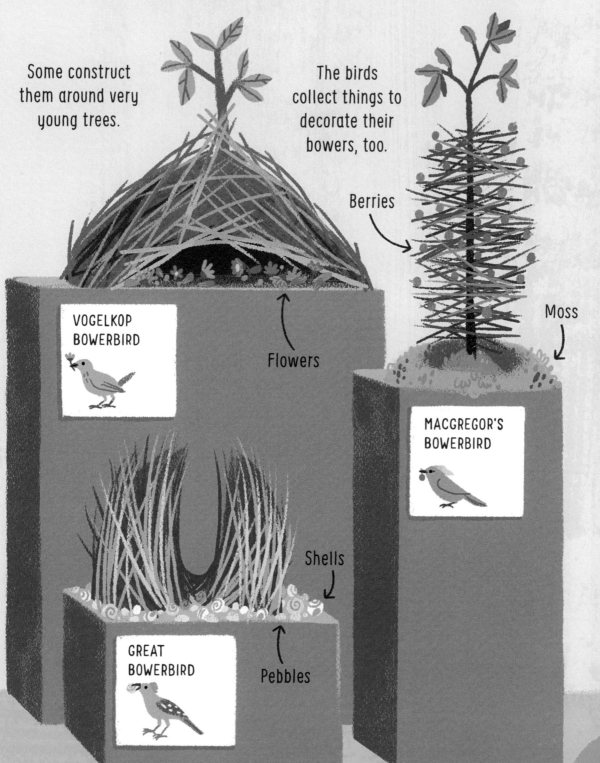

Some construct them around very young trees.

The birds collect things to decorate their bowers, too.

Berries

Moss

VOGELKOP BOWERBIRD

MACGREGOR'S BOWERBIRD

Flowers

Shells

GREAT BOWERBIRD

Pebbles

Whose bones?

If you could look inside different animals with the help of a giant X-ray machine, you'd see pictures like these...

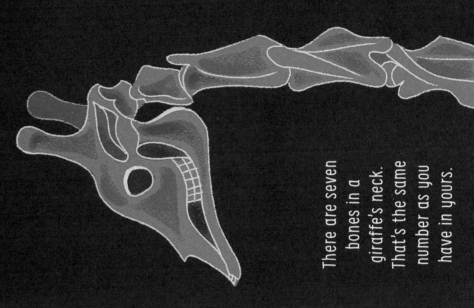

Find the two tall bumps on top of this giraffe's skull. They're called *ossicones.*

There are seven bones in a giraffe's neck. That's the same number as you have in yours.

Snakes' skeletons are mostly made up of just two kinds of bones — but they can have *hundreds* of each.

VERTEBRAE

RIBS

Beavers' tails are wide and flat to help them to steer while swimming. But there's only a thin row of bones through the middle.

(Giraffe neck bones are much, much *longer* than human ones of course.)

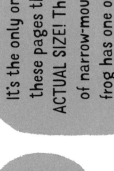

It's the only one on these pages that's ACTUAL SIZE! This type of narrow-mouthed frog has one of the smallest skeletons in the world.

What about this tiny X-ray?

An elephant's trunk disappears on X-rays because it's *boneless*.

This is a bat's thumb bone.

The four spindly bones that stretch to the tips of the wing are fingers.

Is it a bird? No — it's the skull of a blue whale.

Polar bear names

Polar bears are called **polar** bears because they live on sea ice near the North **Pole**. But there are other words for this creature from around the world and long ago...

Nanuk

White sea deer

Old man in the fur cloak

White bear

Ursus maritimus

Rider of icebergs

Ice bear

Err... What does *Ursus maritimus* mean?

That's its scientific name. It's made up of the words for BEAR and SEA in a language called Latin.

Celebrity animals

Several kinds of animals are named after famous people. Look closely at the scientific names and find out who's who.

Please may I have your autograph?

Spheniscus humboldti
German explorer Alexander von Humboldt

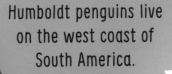

Humboldt penguins live on the west coast of South America.

Zaglossus attenboroughi
British TV presenter David Attenborough

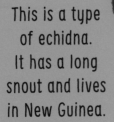

This is a type of echidna. It has a long snout and lives in New Guinea.

This type of spider is found in South Africa.

Stasimopus mandelai
South African leader Nelson Mandela

Scaptia beyonceae
American singer Beyoncé

This Australian horse fly has golden hairs at the tip of its body.

Scientists discovered this tiny snail in the forests of Brunei.

Craspedotropis gretathunbergae
Swedish campaigner Greta Thunberg

Why sleeping sea otters sometimes hold paws

Sea otters spend almost all their time in water – even when they're asleep.

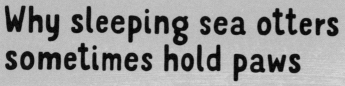

Before going to sleep, a sea otter wraps itself in kelp plants so it won't float away.

And pairs of otters hold paws to make sure they don't **drift apart**.

Kelp is a type of large seaweed that grows up from the ocean floor.

Shhh! These animals are all fast asleep too...

After a big meal, Komodo dragons — the largest lizards in the world — sleep for as much as a **whole week**.

That's 168 hours.

Sperm whales sleep **upright**, with their tails pointing down.

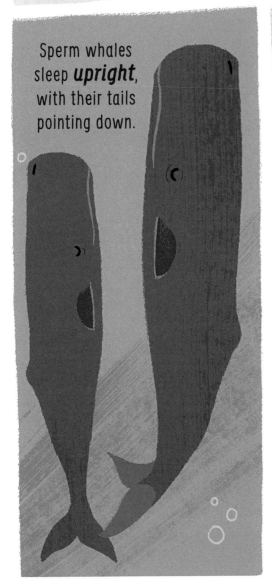

Sea birds called great frigatebirds can sleep while **gliding** in mid-air.

Giraffes, zebras and elephants can all sleep and stay **standing up**.

Glossary

Here you can find out what some of the words in this book *mean*...

algae – tiny plants that grow in water or damp places

Antarctic – the icy land and sea near the South Pole

antifreeze – a chemical that stops something from freezing

Arctic – the icy land and sea near the North Pole

blowhole – a breathing hole on top of a whale's head

blubber – a thick layer of fat under the skin of seals and whales

bower – a pretty structure of twigs or grasses made by bowerbirds

burrow – a hole or tunnel in the ground where some animals live

corals – sea creatures that form rock-like structures

fangs – sharp, pointed teeth

fins – flat parts of a fish, whale or dolphin's body that stick out

gills – body parts that fish and some animals have for breathing underwater

kelp – a large type of seaweed

migration – a journey made by animals in search of food, better weather and places to have babies

moss – a soft, springy plant that grows on rocks and tree bark

muscle – a body part used for moving

ossicones – bony bumps on a giraffe's head

ribs – thin, curved bones

rosette – a flower-shaped spot

scales – little parts over an animal's skin or wings that protect its body

school – a group of fish swimming in the same direction

shed – to lose a layer of skin or sometimes another body part

silk – a fine, sticky thread made by spiders and some baby insects

sponge – a living thing with lots of holes that grows on the sea floor

swarm – a group of flying animals

trench – a deep crack in the ground or sea floor

venom – a type of poison that some animals use to kill, stun or blind other animals

vertebrae – small bones that join together to make up the backbone

Index

Series editor: Ruth Brocklehurst
Series designer: Stephen Moncrieff

First published in 2022 by Usborne Publishing Ltd., 83-85 Saffron Hill, London EC1N 8RT,
United Kingdom. usborne.com Copyright © 2022 Usborne Publishing Ltd. The name Usborne
and the Balloon logo are Trademarks of Usborne Publishing Ltd. All rights reserved. No part
of this publication may be reproduced, stored in any retrievable system, or transmitted in
any form or by any means, without the prior permission of the publisher. UKE.